Kids vs. Nature

Book 2

Surviving
Desert View

Written by:
Karl Steam

Illustrated by:
Joshua Lagman

For the children of San Carlos.

ISBN: 978-1-63578-008-6
Printed and bound in the United States
First Edition

Current contact information for Karl Steam can be found at
www.karlsteam.com

Contents

Surviving
Desert View

Chapter 0
Yea, Chapter 0. Get Over It.

The day before, my teacher had stuck me in a group with Melisa (the nerd), Tyler (the loser), and Katie (the beautiful). To help us finish our assignment, we downloaded a nature identification app, called The Firefly Missions, but as soon as it installed on Katie's phone, it transported us to a forest and wouldn't let us return home until we took a picture of a moose.

Well, long story short, we got the picture, but only after surviving a night in the woods. The app transported us back to class, but it was like we had never left. So, we promised not to tell anyone about our wilderness slumber party. They wouldn't have believed us anyways.

We thought our little adventure had been a one-time deal, but it wasn't. It happened again, the very next day.

Chapter 1
Here We Go Again

We were sitting at our desks, listening to Mrs. Emmons lecture about our graduation ceremony. The more she talked, the more I wished I didn't have to attend the ceremony. Who'd want to walk in front of a crowded gym, just to shake the principal's hand, and get a rolled-up piece of paper? Not me.

The worst part was, after the graduation, there would be the 6th grade dance. It might not sound that bad, but the way I see it, I'd have to stay at school even longer, while the younger grades could go home and start their summer vacations early.

To make things even worse, my mom is really excited about the graduation and dance and wants to take me shopping, so that she can buy me a "special outfit" to wear. Sounds ridiculous, I know.

Usually, I drift into daydreams on accident during class. This time, I was trying to daydream, but no matter how hard I tried, Mrs. Emmons' whiny voice kept pulling me back into reality. It didn't help that John was leaning forward in his seat and gently touching the back of Tyler's neck with a sheet of paper. Every time the paper grazed Tyler's skin, John pulled his arm back and straightened in his seat. Then he'd grin when Tyler scratched at the spot.

John was leaning forward another time when a pulse of light appeared.

Before my eyes opened again, I knew I wasn't in the classroom anymore. I could hear Mrs. Emmons voice cut out mid-sentence, mid-word even. "Principal Gilton will call your name. You'll walk to the front of the gym, shake her hand, and I'll be th..."

When my eyes did open, I was expecting to see a forest and a lake, like the last time. Well, let's just say that expectation was a little off.

Chapter 2
No Trees, No Problem.
No Lake, BIG Problem.

The glowing smoke faded away. Cactuses were all around us. We were sitting in a circle again, but this time we were on top of rocky soil. We were back in our black t-shirts and leather hiking shoes. The only thing different was that we were wearing jean shorts instead of pants.

"What the heck Katie," Melisa said.

Katie stood up, brushing tan dust from her legs. "Don't get all mad at me. I didn't do anything."

Melisa crossed her arms. "Well, who else has the app on their phone?"

"It's been in my pocket the whole time. "To prove it, Katie pulled the phone halfway out of her pocket, before slipping it in again. "Do you think I like getting stuck with you guys?"

"At least no one can blame me this time," Tyler said.

"What do we have to do to get back?" Melisa asked.

Katie turned the phone on and tapped the screen. The rest of us moved closer to see what the mission was going to be.

"What kind of bird do you think it is?" Tyler asked.

"No, a bird's eye view," Melisa said. "I think we just need to get a bird's perspective when flying."

"We need to get high off the ground," I tried to explain, because Tyler still looked confused.

"Or get on top of something really tall," Katie added and pointed behind me.

I turned and saw a big rock poking out of the ground. Okay, the rock was more like a mountain, but not the kind you're probably thinking of. When I think of mountains, I picture a pointy, snow covered, skiing mountain. You know, with sloping sides. This one seriously looked like a massive rock had smashed out of the earth. It was flat on top with jagged cliff edges that rose straight from the ground. Even if there was snow, you couldn't have skied down it. One step off the top would be like stepping off a skyscraper.

I guess I was just standing there, staring when Tyler moved past me. "Hey, there were only two last time," Tyler said. He walked in the direction of the mountain but stopped in front of a little cactus. There were canteens hanging off of it, four canteens to be exact. Resting against the base of the cactus was that weird looking backpack too.

Katie walked up to the cactus. "Great, so it knows there're four of us." She pulled the strap of a canteen away from the needles, unscrewed the cover, and turned it upside down. Not a drop came out.

Tyler opened the backpack, which had the pot, matches, knife, and ropes inside.

Katie put the canteen strap over her shoulder and walked toward the mountain. "Let's get this over with," she said.

Melisa leaned close to me. "This isn't good," she whispered. "We'll need water."

Chapter 3
Cactus, Cactus, Highway

We weaved our way around the cactuses. Katie took pictures of a few. I recognized the tall ones, which the app called Saguaro cactuses. They're the ones usually seen on TV with an arm growing on each side. In real life, they look a little different though. They usually have tons of arms sprouting out or none at all. No two saguaros looked the same.

Katie came to a stop. "These things are getting really annoying," she said.

Some of the smaller cactuses, called prickly pears, were constantly in our way. They're the ones that look like a bunch of ovals stacked on top of one another. The problem was they grew

so close together that they sometimes made me feel like we were in a giant maze. We'd walk around huge clumps of them, just to run into a dead-end. Then we'd need to find our way back and look for a different path to the mountain.

"Perfect," Katie said. She stepped over a cactus arm and into a dry sandy stream bed. It seemed to lead toward the mountain, so we used it like a path. Well, more like a road. We were able to walk a lot faster in the stream bed because cactuses didn't grow there. It was like our own desert highway.

Chapter 4
Who's the Boss

A lizard scurried and ran under a stone near Katie's feet. She screamed, then covered her mouth. "Gross. You guys, I don't want to be here anymore."

"It's okay," I said because I thought she might cry. "It's probably more afraid of you than you are of it."

Tyler hurried to the rock. It was his turn to carry the backpack, so the pot clanked with each of his strides. He put his hands on the rock and tried lifting.

"Don't," Katie shouted. "Leave it alone."

Tyler took a step back. He held his hands up, as if under arrest. "I wasn't going to hurt it," he said. "I want to see if I can catch it."

Katie put a hand over her mouth. "Don't. That's just gross."

"Hey, let me go first," I said. "I'll scare all the lizards off the trail for you."

Katie nodded, and I took the lead. My idea wasn't really to scare the lizards out of the way. I was thinking more like Tyler. I wanted to catch one too. If Katie were in the lead, she'd scream and scare them away, before I had a chance to sneak up on them.

It wasn't long before another lizard ran from the stream bed. I slowed and tried to creep closer, but it scurried further away.

Tyler pushed his way in front of me. "Why do you get to catch them and I can't?"

"You guys, knock it off. We don't have time to goof around," Melisa said.

"Why not?" I asked. "When will we ever have the chance to catch a lizard again?"

"But we have to get back home," she said.

"Why? We've been there a thousand times before. Have you ever seen a desert?" I asked. "We know what we have to do to get back. Let's have fun while we're here."

"Yea," Tyler said. "We should explore."

"No. It's my phone, and I say we keep going," Katie said.

Melisa put her hands on her hips. "Since when did that make you the boss?"

"Okay, I'm not the boss," Katie said, "but it's getting hot. We can't stay here."

Melisa relaxed. Her arms fell back to her sides. "How about you two just explore on the way to the mountain," she suggested to me and Tyler.

"Deal," I said. "Let's have some fun you guys. This is going to be a once in a lifetime opportunity."

"It better be," Katie mumbled.

Chapter 5
Disgusting

I'll be the first to admit that catching a lizard isn't easy. Unlike moose, they're hard to sneak up on.

Me and Tyler decided to hunt together, like a pack. We took turns circling each lizard, trying to scare them toward the other person. Sometimes this actually worked, but even then, it was hard to catch them. Every time I dove at one, it scurried beyond my reach.

We finally found this crazy looking lizard that had spikes growing out of its body. It was also fat compared to the others. It didn't seem to run as fast and only went a short way before stopping to rest.

I had to dive into the sand a couple times but eventually caught it with one hand.

"Alright," Tyler said, as the lizard tried to squirm away. "You got 'em."

I was about to hang onto the lizard with my other hand too when the most disgusting thing happened. It looked like its eyeballs exploded. A stream of red liquid went shooting from its eyes right onto my shoulder and the side of my face. A few drops fell onto the hand I was holding it with too.

"Don't squeeze so hard," Tyler shouted. "You're killing it."

I let go. The lizard scurried away, then stopped to rest again.

Katie and Melisa ran closer.

"I hardly squeezed it," I said. "It just squirted out."

"Maybe it's poison," Tyler said.

I didn't think any of it hit my mouth, but I started spitting just to make sure I wouldn't swallow any.

"Can I see the phone?" Melisa asked.

Katie gave it to her and Melisa carefully stepped closer to the lizard. The electronic click could be heard as she took its picture.

"Analyzing image," the app said. "Horned Lizard."

Melisa silently read the app's description of a horned lizard.

"Well, is it poison?" I asked.

"No. It says that they can squirt blood from their eyes when they feel threatened. It's supposed to scare away predators."

I tried to wipe the blood from my shoulder. Without water to clean it off, it just smeared around. The sight made me feel like barfing.

"I told you guys to leave them alone," Katie said.

Chapter 6
Oasis

We traveled faster once me and Tyler lost the desire to catch lizards. The ground became hilly, and the closer we came to the mountain, the more gigantic it seemed.

"Hey, trees," Melisa said.

Further up the stream bed, trees were growing where two hills merged. "Grass too. Green grass." I added since grass had withered and tanned everywhere else.

Trees and green grass could only mean one thing—water. Melisa and I ran ahead, but the stream bed still only had sand and rocks on it.

"Anything there?" Tyler yelled.

"It's dry," I called back.

"There might still be water," Melisa said. She walked to the middle of the grass and kicked at the sand. "Help me dig. Their roots have to be getting water somehow."

We knelt and scooped sand away. A pit grew deeper and deeper. The sand began to feel cool, and it looked darker too. Eventually, it felt wet and stuck together in clumps. Finally, our fingertips touched water. We dug the edges of the pit wider, and soon there was a small puddle. I cupped some water in my hands and cleaned the lizard blood from my face. Melisa kept digging until the puddle was big enough for a canteen to fit inside.

By now Katie and Tyler were there too. Tyler took the backpack off.

When Melisa's canteen was done filling, she put the cover back on. "Give me another," she said.

I passed my canteen to her. "How do you know it's safe to drink?" I asked. "It looks really dirty."

"I don't," Melisa said. "We'll have to purify it first."

"What do you mean?"

"We need to boil it to kill any bacteria living in the water."

"And how do you know that'll work?" Katie asked.

"Look, after we made it back from the moose mission, I decided to do some research. We were all pretty clueless about how to survive in the wilderness," Melisa said. "One of the things I read is that if you boil water for at least ten minutes, it should be safe to drink. That's how I learned to dig in the ground for water too."

"So, you thought the app would send us somewhere again?" Katie asked.

Melisa shook her head. "No, but I still wanted to be better prepared in case I'd ever get stranded somewhere else. You know, like if my car broke down in the middle of nowhere."

"We'll have to start another fire," Tyler said. He unzipped the backpack and pulled out the box of matches.

Chapter 7
Boiling Time

Well, finding firewood was a lot harder in the desert than in the forest. Since there were only a few trees growing between the hills, we were only able to find a couple dead branches. After that, we had to look for dead shrubs and grass. Every once in a while, we found the skeleton of a dead cactus, which burned well too, but we had to look all over to find a good supply for the fire.

Tyler eventually struck a match and lowered it to our pile of wood. As the flames grew larger, we set the canteens in a circle around the fire. After that, we waited, and waited, and waited.

Man, it seemed to take forever for the water in those canteens to boil. Sitting there waiting was really boring too, almost as boring as Mrs. Emmons' class.

At least it was, until Tyler said, "Look at that."

Next to one of the tree trunks was the biggest spider I had ever seen.

"I really hate this place," Katie said. She took out her phone and snapped a picture.

"Analyzing image... Tarantula."

Katie turned to me. "You guys kill it or something."

"No," Melisa said, "It's a wild animal."

"So are the spiders that sometimes crawl into homes and people kill them," Katie said. "What's the difference?"

"Aren't they poisonous?" I asked.

Melisa and Katie leaned over the phone to read the information about tarantulas.

"It's not hurting anybody," Melisa said, as she was reading. Melisa pointed at the bottom of the screen. "There, it says they're poisonous, but not enough to kill a person. It just hurts a lot when they bite."

"Well, keep it away from here," Katie said.

One of the canteens began to boil.

"Finally," I said.

Melisa moved the canteen a little further away from the fire so that the water inside wouldn't boil over the top.

"Hey, let's scare it away," Tyler said to me.

We whispered together and counted to three. "One... Two... Three."

Chapter 8
Who's Scared Now?

We charged at the spider. When we got close, it twitched, but otherwise stayed where it was. We took turns getting a little closer. We stomped our feet. The tarantula stood its ground.

"Rrraaah" Tyler yelled, jumping closer yet. The spider raised its front legs into the air.

"You're making it mad," Katie warned.

"Yea, maybe just keep an eye on it and tell us if it comes this way," Melisa said.

So that's what me and Tyler did. We watched it sit there, and sit there. After a while, it was almost as boring as watching the water in our canteens boil. You'd think a spider would have better things to do than just stay in one place for such a long time.

A buzzing noise came close to our heads. Tyler and I ducked. I was expecting a bee, but it was a hummingbird. It hovered above us, zooming one way, then the other way. Finally, it flew to a tree and rested on a branch.

Its long beak turned from one direction to the other as it looked around. Soon a second hummingbird came buzzing by but didn't stop. When the first bird noticed, it rose straight up from the branch like a helicopter would. Then it flew off to chase the other one.

"That's cool," I said. "You really can't see their wings moving."

"Hey, where'd it go?" Tyler asked.

I glanced back at the ground. The tarantula was gone. It wasn't by the tree trunk. It wasn't on top of the sand. I jumped back to see if it was by my feet. It wasn't. Tyler and I looked at each other, then ran back to the fire.

"We don't know where it is," Tyler said. He glanced at the tree again.

"What do you mean you don't know where it is?" Melisa asked.

"We lost it," I said.

Katie picked up the strap for her canteen and pulled it from the fire. She ran but held the canteen away from her body so the hot metal wouldn't brush against her leg. Tyler was the next person to grab his canteen, and soon me and Melisa were running with ours. Since I was technically the last person to leave, I was stuck carrying the backpack too.

Chapter 9
The Mountain

You know how people say not to look down when you're climbing something tall? Well, when it comes to mountain climbing, I found it better not to look up. Yea the mountain looked big from a distance, but now that we were closer, it was humungous.

I didn't tell the others, but I was getting scared, real scared. Like, sick to my stomach. The way you feel before riding a rollercoaster the first time. I wasn't sure if an experienced climber would even try this mountain.

When we reached the base, the climb became steep and the ground rocky. Sometimes, we crossed giant slabs of stone. Since fewer cactuses grew in these rocky areas, we were able to leave the streambed and pick our own path up the mountain.

"Watch it," Melisa said, as Tyler's foot slipped on some gravel. He was standing and trying to walk uphill, while Melisa was using her hands and feet. "If you start sliding, it'll be really hard to stop yourself," she warned.

I looked behind us. It was a long way to tumble, and we were guaranteed to hit a few cactuses on the way down. I wondered what it would feel like to run into a cactus at high speeds. Surely the needles would push far into our bodies. I figured that even if a person closed their eyes before hitting them, the needles would probably poke right through their eyelids. That's why I planned to cover my face if I did start rolling.

I lowered myself down to all fours and crawled like Melisa. I felt a lot more stable once some weight was resting on my hands.

Tyler kept standing. He gazed up, one hand above his eyes to block the sun. "Do you think they're waiting for one of us to fall?" he asked, referring to the vultures circling overhead.

"Just you," Katie said, "unless you start crawling like the rest of us."

Chapter 10
Crawling

Have you ever been in a shopping mall and dared by your friend to run up the escalator that brings people down? I have, and trust me, you are one tired puppy by the time you make it to the top. Even though you're running as fast as you can, you only move a little ways because it's constantly pulling you back down.

Well, sometimes that's how climbing the mountain felt. Parts of the incline were completely covered with small rocks, so every time we climbed forward, we slid backward a ways too. It was like rolling on a bunch of tiny marbles back down the mountain, which meant we had to work extra hard to climb even a little higher.

The sun was high in the sky now. It was getting warm, really warm. I started to drink some of my water, which was no longer boiling hot. I only took a few sips here and there, because I knew I should save most of it for later.

We finally made it up the incline and to the base of the cliff. Now the real climbing would begin. Or at least that's what I thought.

"How are we supposed to get up this thing," Katie asked, as she ran her hand along the stone wall. There wasn't a single crack or ledge to grab hold of.

Chapter 11
The Cliff

We sat, our backs resting against the rock wall. Our sleeves were rolled up, turning our T-shirts into muscle shirts. I would've taken off my whole shirt if it weren't for the cactuses. With my luck, I would probably brush against one as soon as I didn't have a shirt on to protect my skin.

I looked at how high we had climbed. The trees, where we had seen the tarantula, looked itty bitty now.

Remembering the tarantula made me think of something.

"Hey Katie, can you look up scorpions?" I asked. "Are they like tarantulas and only hurt if they sting, or can they actually kill?"

I could tell the question made Katie nervous. She started looking at the rocks close by to see if any scorpions were near.

"I'll look it up," Melisa offered. She searched a while then shook her head. "There are lots of different kinds. Most of them will just hurt bad, but some can kill. The good thing is they like to hide during the day and usually only come out at night when it's cooler out."

"We better not be here over night," Katie said. "Raccoons were bad enough. I'm not dealing with scorpions."

"You guys, we're never going to be able to climb these walls," I said. "Do you think there's a way up on the other side?"

"I'm not crawling all the way back down there," Tyler said.

I could tell he was hot because he was sweating more than the rest of us and his face was redder than normal too."

"We might not need to," Melisa said. "I think we should've stayed in that stream bed." She pointed further along the mountain, toward the top. "See that V shape at the edge of the cliff?" she asked. "It looks like that's where the stream runs down the side of the mountain. It's worn away some of the cliff so that it's not as steep there."

"I think you're right," I said.

I could see the V shape that Melisa was talking about, and it looked like water had eroded a groove from the top of the cliff all the way down to the base.

Katie was the first to stand. She walked by the cliff's wall, heading for the stream's groove.

Me and Melisa stood up too.

"Can't we rest a little longer?" Tyler asked. He continued to lean against the cliff.

"Do whatever you want," Katie said, without breaking stride or even turning around. "But, I'm making it to the top before nighttime."

"Same here," Melisa said.

I waited as Tyler stood up and we followed the girls around the side of the mountain.

Chapter 12
The Real Climbing Begins

It took quite a while to get to the groove the stream had made. What had seemed like ordinary rocks from a distance, turned out to be giant boulders up close. Sometimes they were so tall, we couldn't even jump up and reach the top of them. Instead, we had to climb between their crevices. It was a lot of work and slow going, but we were making progress up the mountain.

Melisa crossed her arms and waited for Katie to pull herself onto the next rock ledge. "Can you go any faster," she complained.

"Just relax, will you. It's tougher than it looks," Katie said.

"Oh yea?" Melisa climbed up the rock as if she were a squirrel. "This is going to take forever if we keep going at your speed."

Melisa climbed past Katie, who was struggling to find a good place for her hands to grab onto the next rock. Katie stepped to the side so that I could climb around her too. After managing to pull myself on top of the stone, I leaned over the side to help Katie.

Helping her didn't seem like a big deal at first, but that changed as soon as her hand touched mine. I hadn't ever held hands with a girl before, let alone a girl as good looking as Katie.

It was exciting and scary at the same time. I felt weak, so I started to use both of my hands to hold onto her. The last thing I wanted to do was ruin the moment by dropping her.

"Thanks," Katie said after she stood up.

I climbed the next rock, planning to help her onto that one too. Then I realized I had touched her with my "lizard blood hand." I mean, I had washed my hand when we found water, but even still I didn't want to risk ruining the moment by grossing Katie out, so I decided to let her climb on her own after that.

Chapter 13
Collapse

A long time later, my arms grew tired and my shirt sagged with sweat. I couldn't keep up with Melisa, even if my life depended on it. I hoped it never would. I wondered if her climbing ability had something to do with her being the shortest person in the group which meant less bodyweight pulling her down. Maybe that made it easier for her to climb than us bigger people. It was Tyler that I felt bad for. He was the biggest one of all.

I hadn't heard Tyler in a while, which was a little different for him. Usually, his feet would be dragging against the ground behind me, or he'd be talking about something.

I turned to see where he was. He was climbing the next level of rocks. His arms shook, and his face was pale. He finally pulled himself over the top, or maybe it'd be better to say that he just kind of rolled onto the top. He must have been holding his breath while he was pulling himself up because he laid on his back and started to breathe really fast. Not great deep breaths, but lots of shorter breaths.

I waited before calling to him.

"Tyler, are you alright?"

I must have woken him from a trance. He tried standing, but couldn't. He wobbled to the side and collapsed onto the rocks.

Chapter 14
Hot

"Tyler!" I shouted. I pulled the backpack's straps off my shoulders and let it drop to the ground. "Don't move!"

I dashed away from the rock I was about to climb, slid down a few others, and went past Katie. I hated climbing down the mountain. It meant I would need to climb right back up again, but I knew Tyler needed me.

"What's wrong?" Melisa called after I reached Tyler.

I didn't answer her because I didn't know the answer. I figured he was thirsty and picked up his canteen. It was empty. I was expecting his shirt to be all sweaty like mine, but it actually seemed dry. He didn't even have sweat drops forming on his forehead.

"Tyler, are you alright?" I asked.

Of course, I knew he wasn't, but didn't know what else to say. Finally, I thought of something a little better. "Hey, what's wrong?"

Tyler gently shook his head. "I feel like throwing up."

Katie was next to me now. "Tyler you have to drink something," she said. "This happened to one of the girls on my soccer team last summer. You're dehydrated." Katie glanced at me. "Help me sit him up."

We each grabbed one of Tyler's shoulders and helped him sit.

I put my canteen in his hands. "Tyler, you have to drink," I repeated.

Tyler held the canteen, but his grip was weak. I helped him lift it to his lips and didn't let go until he could hold it by himself.

He gulped some of my water. It made me sad to see him drink it. Believe me, I was thirsty too and was working hard to save most of my water for later. At the same time, I knew giving it to him was the right thing to do.

We sat with him a while, letting him rest.

"Is he alright?" Melisa asked.

She had been quite a way higher on the mountain but had climbed down to help too.

I shrugged. "He's looking a little better."

It was true. Giving him some water and time to rest seemed to give him a little strength back. He could at least sit up on his own now without me and Katie helping.

"We should get him out of the sun," Melisa said. "There's a cave a little way further, if he can make it that far."

We gave Tyler a few more minutes and a few more drinks from our canteens. Then we continued climbing. Katie and I each held onto Tyler so that he wouldn't fall again. Melisa picked up the backpack where I had dropped it, put it on her shoulders, and led the way.

Tyler climbed the best he could. We helped to push and pull him the best we could.

Eventually, we made it high enough to get to the cave Melisa was talking about.

The cave was not that deep. It was actually more like a wide overhang that had formed. Even still, I could feel cooler air just by taking a few steps into the cave. It was definitely nice to get out of the sun.

"I think it was a mistake trying to climb during the middle of the afternoon," Melisa said. "We should've learned from the scorpions. They know better than to come out during the heat of the day. We should wait until it's a little cooler before we keep going."

Me and Katie were still tired from helping Tyler climb, so we just nodded.

Chapter 15
Time to Rest

"I think we're over halfway there," Melisa said.

We were sitting at the edge of the cave, and looking out over the mountain.

The vultures that had been soaring above us were not as small anymore. At first, I thought they must have seen Tyler fall over and were flying lower so that they could eventually start eating him. After a while, I realized they didn't seem to be following us. They were just closer now because we had climbed up so much higher. We were the ones that had gotten closer to them.

"I'm going to have the worst tan line ever," Katie said.

She was holding the neck of her T-shirt over her shoulder so that she could look at her skin. There was a strip of light skin that went over the top of Katie's shoulder. That was where her sleeves had been rolled up while we were climbing. The rest of her skin was turning darker every minute.

Melisa showed us the red skin on her shoulder. "Mine are burn lines. I'm keeping my sleeves unrolled from here on out."

My shoulders were burnt just as bad. Good thing I didn't take my shirt off earlier. If I had, my entire upper body would have been stinging with pain.

I watched Tyler take another sip of water. We had each chipped in and poured some of our water into his canteen. Hopefully, it'd be enough to keep him from getting dehydrated again. Hopefully, we'd all have enough.

My stomach gurgled. As thirsty as I was, I
think I was even hungrier. There weren't
exactly patches of blueberries growing in the
desert like there was in the forest. It hadn't
really hit me while we were climbing. I think I
was just concentrating on the hard work. Now
that we were lying still, my stomach was trying
to get my attention.

I hoped the day would cool off soon, so we
could start climbing again. I wondered if all
the other desert animals that hide in the
shade during the day feel as restless as I did.
They probably wanted to get up, move around,
and find something to eat too.

Chapter 16
Sunset

The sky showed faint shades of orange and pink as the sun sank closer to the horizon. Even the rocks on the mountain seemed to look a tad orange as the light hit them and caused long shadows to form.

We left the cave as soon as the air outside began to cool.

"Let's move fast you guys. We probably only have a couple hours of light left." Melisa said. "And who knows if we'll be able to see much once it's dark."

Melisa still carried the backpack. She led us up the mountain. This time, Katie stayed in the back, since she seemed to be the slowest. Well, Tyler was still the slowest, but we wanted someone to stay behind him in case anything would happen again.

Since we had just been resting, I had quite a bit of energy. I wanted to get as much climbing done before I started to tire out.

I looked behind me to see how Tyler and Katie were doing. They were a ways behind, but still climbing well. It was then that I saw how high we were. The vultures that had been flying around the cliff walls were still there, but now they were below us. I hadn't even realized that we had climbed higher than them.

"Katie," I called. I pointed to the vultures. "Maybe we're already high enough for the 'bird's eye view.'"

She took out the phone and held it up to take a picture.

Katie shook her head. "It didn't work," she yelled back.

Melisa waited until I caught up with her. Then we both waited for the other two.

The pink colors in the sky had disappeared and were replaced with shades of red. The orange that remained was darkening too.

"We're getting close," Melisa said. "We should be able to make it before it's completely dark."

We followed Melisa again. I really tried to keep up with her this time. It was sort of a challenge, to see if I had learned to climb just as well. I can't say that I kept up with her, but she didn't pull too far ahead of me either.

The red in the sky dimmed, but we were almost to the top. I was about to climb the next layer of rocks when Melisa stopped. She had pulled herself onto a rock but was staying on her hands and knees. The backpack was probably making her tired. Maybe I would catch up with her after all.

I got to the top of one layer and started to climb the next rock when I heard it. A soft hissing noise was coming from somewhere near Melisa.

Chapter 17
Rattle Rattle

Don't ask me how I knew it was a rattlesnake. I could just feel in my gut that a snake was up there, probably all coiled up, shaking its tail, and ready to strike.

"Melisa, you got to get out of there," I said.

"How?" she asked. Her voice sounded weird because she was trying to talk without moving her lips. "It's right next to me."

"Try to scoot back down the way you came."

"It'll bite," she said.

I climbed faster. I didn't know what to do, but I had to do something. My first idea was to throw a rock at it. Maybe that'd distract it or injure it enough for Melisa to get away. Then I remembered our last mission, where a moose taught me a lesson about throwing rocks at animals. Besides, a rock might upset the snake even more and make it strike.

I was close to Melisa. The hissing of the rattle was much louder now. All I had to do was climb the same rock she was on.

I tried to judge where the snake was on the rock so that I wouldn't climb up within striking range. I slowly lifted my head over the edge, and there it was. A big, coiled rattler, just like I imagined. It turned and looked at me for a brief moment, but then focused on Melisa again since she was closest. She was only a few feet away. I was a few yards away.

"I'm going to distract it," I said.

Melisa didn't take her eyes off the snake. She hardly even moved. "Hurry," she mumbled. "Be careful."

I inched closer to the snake and waved my arms to get its attention. I might not know much about most animals, but I know a lot about rattlesnakes. I always thought they were cool and did one of my third-grade research papers on them. So, I knew rattlesnakes not only have regular eyesight, but also infrared sensors that allow them to see body heat. I was moving closer, and it definitely saw me.

Chapter 18
Lightning Speed

The snake was looking right at me. It rattled harder. I stopped moving. I didn't want to get within striking distance, which I knew is usually about half the body length of the snake. The problem was it's hard to judge how long a snake is while it's coiled up. Only one thing was sure; I had its attention.

"You guys. What's wrong?" Katie asked.

We didn't answer.

"Alright, try to scoot back down," I said. "Go slow."

Melisa slowly stretched her legs back down. She pushed her body backward with her arms next. Then she slid her arms back too but had to stop because the snake looked at her again.

"Shoot," I said. "Hang on. We'll try again." I waved my arms some more and tapped my feet against the rock a little. I knew they could feel vibrations in the ground too. I just hoped it would be enough vibrations to get it to look at me again, instead of scaring it enough to bite.

The snake did look at me. Melisa eased herself back some more.

"AAAWWW."

It happened so fast I could hardly see it move. The snake lunged at Melisa. She shrieked, twisted her body, rolled off the rock, and fell to the ground below. I jumped back as far as I could without falling myself. The snake quickly turned and slithered away, disappearing under a pile of stones.

Melisa whimpered and clenched her wrist. It looked like she was holding back tears.

Have you ever had a teacher tell you that, "There is no such thing as a stupid question?" Well, I officially declare that statement wrong, because I asked the same thing I asked Tyler earlier in the day.

"Are you alright?"

Stupid, I know. I just don't know what else to say in these kinds of situations.

"It got me," Melisa said.

Chapter 19
To the Top

There were two red dots on her wrist, where the fangs had pierced the skin. I helped free her arms from the backpack's straps, so she could lay flat on the ground.

"Alright, now stay still," I told her. "The more you move, the faster your heart beats. The faster your heart beats, the more it pumps venom around your body."

Melisa hardly nodded.

"Just take some deep breaths and try to relax," I said.

Katie knew something was wrong. She passed Tyler and was close now.

Melisa sat up, even though I told her not to. "Let's get to the top," she said. "We need to go home... and find help."

I wanted to protest but didn't. She was right. We could spend the night here, trying to keep her alive, or we could get her to a clinic.

Katie lifted her phone and took a picture of the world below. Nothing happened. "I'll go the rest of the way," she said. "You wait here."

"But what if you're too far away from us?" I asked. "What if it takes you home and leaves us behind?"

Melisa stood. "We'll all go," she said. "Technically the rest of us won't complete the mission unless we make it to the top too. The app might not like that," she pointed out. "Let's go."

There were only two climbs left. Melisa seemed okay at first. But climbing made her heart pump faster. The venom spread quickly. Soon, she couldn't even stand on her own.

Tyler caught up with us. He leaned closer to inspect Melisa's swollen arm. "You want me to suck out the poison?" he asked.

"Stay away," Melisa said.

The slow clumsy way she pulled her arm from Tyler proved how weak she was. She was also shivering, despite the heat. Sure, the evening was cooler than the middle of the day, but it was still pretty hot outside.

"Sucking out the venom doesn't work that well," I told Tyler but didn't explain why I knew so much about rattlesnakes.

The top of the mountain looked more like a hill than a peak. Katie made it there first. The rest of us weren't far behind. Melisa's body was completely limp at that point, so I was carrying her by the armpits and Tyler held her legs.

Katie took a picture of the Earth below. Only a red glow was left on the horizon. It seemed to give all the rocks and cactuses a deep red color. We could see farther than I had ever seen before.

"Analyzing image..."

I held my breath.

"Bird's Eye View... Mission complete," the voice said. "Returning home in one minute..."

The firefly appeared on the screen. I exhaled a sigh of relief. "We did it guys."

There was no cheering or high five giving, like last time. We were happy but too tired to celebrate. Instead, we laid Melisa on the ground and sat beside her.

"Returning home in 45 seconds..."

I wondered how high we had climbed. I wondered if we would even be able to see a house from on top. I certainly couldn't see the trees that we filled up the canteens by or any of the tall saguaro cactuses that we had walked past. They were all too small to recognize. Even a football field might have been hard to notice.

"Returning home in 30 seconds..."

"Melisa?" Tyler tapped her shoulder. Her eyes were closed.

"Hmmm," she said and looked around before closing her eyes again.

"Hey, we're almost back," I said.

"Yea, hold on a little longer," Tyler urged.

"Don't go to sleep," Katie said. "Keep talking to us."

The light on the firefly's tail began to blink on and off. "Returning in 15 seconds...," the voice said.

Melisa didn't say anything.

Tyler shook her shoulder.

Melisa moaned.

"Leave her alone," Katie said. "You might be hurting her."

"Just a few more seconds," Tyler told Melisa.

The light from the firefly's tail grew brighter and brighter.

"Returning in 5... 4... 3... 2... 1..."

The whole screen began to glow. Then a pulse of light sprang from the phone, forcing my eyes to shut.

Chapter 20
We're Back

The next moment, my eyes opened. I was back in Mrs. Emmons' room. She was still droning on about graduation.

"...ere to hand you a carnation. Then you can go back to your seat. After the ceremony is over..."

I looked around. Students were still in their seats. It was like nothing had ever happened. I glanced at the clock. It was 9:42 am.

Melisa came to mind. She was at her desk, looking at her wrist and rubbing it with her hand. It was hard to see if the little red dots were there anymore. Then I noticed her wrist was no longer swollen, so I figured the dots were probably gone too.

Melisa turned and smiled, letting me know she was alright. Then she made eye contact with Tyler and Katie too.

Katie's tan lines were gone. She was also looking at Melisa, but only out of the corner of her eyes. She was trying not to draw too much attention to herself.

Tyler raised his hand. John was about to touch the back of Tyler's neck with a piece of paper, so he pulled his arm back. John sat up straight and dropped the paper too. The smirk that had been on his face was gone.

Katie also sat up straighter. Her back stiffened. I felt nervous too. Was Tyler really going to tell Mrs. Emmons what happened? Nobody would ever believe we were in the desert, had climbed a mountain, or that I had been squirted with lizard blood. Getting anyone to believe that Melisa was bitten by a rattlesnake was out of the question, especially since she didn't have a bite mark to prove it.

Mrs. Emmons paused. "Yes, Tyler?"

"May I please get a drink?"

"Can't you wait?"

"My throat is really dry," Tyler said. "Ehh Hhemm. It's kind of scratchy."

"Go quickly," she said.

Tyler grinned at me, then walked past my desk and out the classroom door.

Chapter 21
Crack

I know I don't pay as much attention in school as I should, but I have to admit that it is a lot harder to focus after such an eventful day. The final bell eventually rang, and a tidal wave of students gushed into the hallway. I met up with Mark, and we moved with the flow of the others to the main doors.

"Hey. Meet me outside," Melisa called to me. "We need to talk."

I nodded as softly as I could so that nobody else would notice. Melisa turned and yelled to Tyler.

"Was she talking to you?" Mark asked. "What's that about?"

"Nothing," I said.

"Are we going to shoot hoops tonight?" Mark asked.

"Yea, just call when you're ready," I said and held my hand into the air.

I wouldn't say that Mark and I have a secret handshake or anything. It's just that ever since fourth grade, we usually give each other a high five, then a fist pound when saying bye.

"See you later," he said.

I stumbled out the school doors, down the stairs, and to the sidewalk. Streams of students rushed past me as I tried to find a quieter place to wait for the others. Soon, Tyler and Melisa joined me near the flagpole.

"We have to figure out how to stop this," Melisa said. "Have you guys seen Katie?"

Tyler pointed to the doors. Katie was just leaving the school.

"Katie," Melisa yelled and waved an arm in the air.

Katie looked around to see if anyone else saw Melisa calling her. She walked over to us. "What do you want?"

"We've got to stop this," Melisa said. "We can't do any more missions like that."

"I know," Katie said. She took out her phone and turned it on.

She raised her arm. Me and Tyler jumped back when we realized what she was doing. She pulled her arm down fast and flung the phone onto the sidewalk.

Katie bent down. She picked it up. There was a crack across the screen. She pushed the power button, but the screen didn't light up. It didn't do anything.

"No more missions," she said and walked to the edge of the sidewalk.

A woman driving a red convertible came to a quick stop. "Hi sweet heart," the woman said to Katie.

As soon as Katie sat down in the car, the woman revved the engine, and they sped away.

"So I guess it's over with," I said.

"I guess so," Melisa agreed.

Chapter 22
The Phone Call

"Anything exciting happen at school today?" my dad asked.

It was the same question every supper.

"Nope."

That was the same answer I tried to give every evening too.

My mom swallowed her bite of potato. "You must be learning something new."

"Josh has some new friends," Molly said.

Molly is my little sister. Sometimes I call her my big sister though because she is a big pain in the butt.

"No, I don't," I said.

"Yea-ha. I saw you with them after school."

"Who are they," Mom asked.

"Nobody," I said, and tried to glare at Molly, but not long enough for Mom and Dad to notice. "I just had to do a group project with them in class. That's all."

"What kind of a project was it?" my dad asked.

"We had corn dogs for lunch today," I said. "That's something exciting, and we got to play basketball in gym class."

I thought my parents were just about ready to stop asking questions when my mom's cell phone rang.

"Hello," Mom said, after unplugging the phone from its charger. "Hang on. He's right here."

I glanced at the clock. Mark must have finished his supper early. Now I was in a hurry to finish eating, so I shoved half of a baked potato in my mouth.

My mom held out the phone for me. "Josh, Katie Roberts wants to talk to you."

Everyone looked at me as I spit the potato back onto my plate. I took the phone from my mom and walked into the other room.

"Hello?"

"Josh, we need to talk."

"What's up?"

"I told my dad that I accidentally dropped my phone today. We have one of those insurance plans on it so that you can replace your phone if it gets damaged. Anyways, he took me to the store to get a new one."

"Yea."

"Well, I checked the phone before we left the store to make sure it didn't have any weird apps on it, if you know what I mean. Well, it didn't, at least not until we got home."

"What are you trying to say?" I asked.

"I just looked at it now, and the app is there," Katie said. "I didn't download it or anything. It just appeared."

"Great," I said, trying to sound sarcastic, but I wasn't. The truth is, I was really thinking, 'this is great.' Not only was I on the phone with Katie Roberts, but I had held her hand earlier in the day too. So, going on another mission actually did sound great.

"Yea, well, I just wanted to let you know that this might not be over," Katie said.

I nodded even though she couldn't see me. "Thanks, I appreciate the heads-up."

"I'm gonna go," she said. "I have to give Melisa and Tyler a heads up too."

"Alright. Have a good night."

"Bye."

I walked back to the kitchen, but even before I made it into the room, Molly said, "Why is Katie Roberts calling you?"

"She had a question about an assignment," I said.

One of Molly's eyebrows lifted. "And she called *you* about it?"

I guess I should have lied better. It was obvious that nobody would be calling me to ask about an assignment, not even Mark. As you already know, I have a tendency to not pay attention in class.

"Just mind your own business Molly."

"Alright you two," dad said. "How about you Molly, anything exciting happen at school today?"

Chapter 23
The Plan

The second phone call came later that night after Mark and I had finished shooting hoops. It was Melisa this time.

"Hi Josh."

"Hey."

"Katie said she told you?"

"Yea."

"Well, I think we need to start taking matters into our own hands."

"You think we can stop it somehow?" I asked.

"I don't know," Melisa said. "I tried looking it up online. It's like the app doesn't even exist. Then when I go to the app store it says that it's sold out. Give me a break, apps don't sell out."

"So what do you want us to do then?" I asked. "The app said it was 'a free one week trial.' We still have five days left."

"Well, we can't just wait around for it to send us to five more places," Melisa said. "We need to start doing some serious research."

"What do you mean?"

"If we're going to make it, we'll have to learn all we can about surviving any kind of wilderness situation."

"Sounds like a plan," I said.

"Oh, and Josh..."

"Yea,"

"Thanks for trying to distract the snake. I mean, I know it didn't work, but thanks for trying."

"No problem. I'm just glad you're alright."

"Okay. Well, have a good night," Melisa said, "and don't forget to do some research."

"I will," I said. "Good night."

👍 Next in the Series

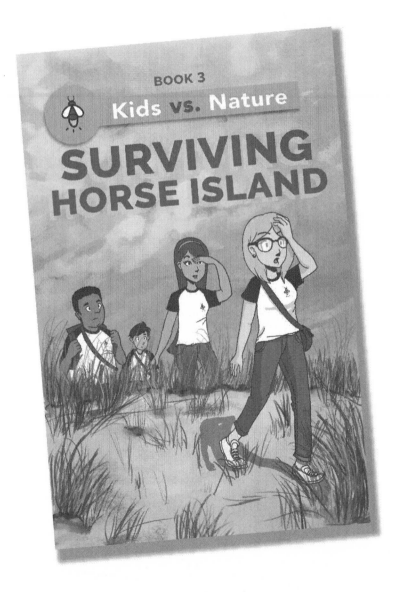

Scenes from Book #3

Fun Facts: Horned Lizards

Do Lizards Really Squirt Blood?

Horned lizards can squirt blood from their eyes. In fact, they can shoot a stream of blood up to three feet away.

You can watch a video of this happening at https://www.karlsteam.com/books/surviving-desert-view/

Why Do They Shoot Blood?

It's a defensive mechanism used to deter predators from eating them. The blood contains chemicals that smell and taste bad, so if a predator gets sprayed with the blood, it often decides to find something more appealing to eat instead.

Does Squirting Blood Hurt Horned Lizards?

No, squirting blood from their eyes does not seem to harm them or their eyesight.

How Do They Do This?

When a horned lizard feels threatened, it builds up blood pressure in the vessels around its eyes. Once the pressure gets too high, a stream of blood is forced out. Picking them up, touching them, or even getting too close can make this happen.

Fun Facts: Hummingbirds

How Fast Do Their Wings Flap?

It depends on the species. According to the U.S. National Park Service, some can flap their wings 80 times a second, but the average North American hummingbird only flaps its wings 53 times a second. Not that 53 times a second is anything to scoff at. It still amounts to over 3000 flaps a minute.

Can you see their wings flap?

When flying, a hummingbird's wings move too fast for a person to see, so they look more like a blur. The best way to see their wing movement is to watch slow motion videos of a hummingbird in flight. www.karlsteam.com/books/surviving-desert-view/ has a sample video for you.

Are They Good Fliers?

They're impressively good. In fact, they're the only bird species that can fly backwards. They can also hover in one place, much like a helicopter.

Why Such Long Beaks?

Long beaks help them to reach the nectar in flowers. They often eat 8 times their body weight in nectar a day to maintain their fast metabolism.

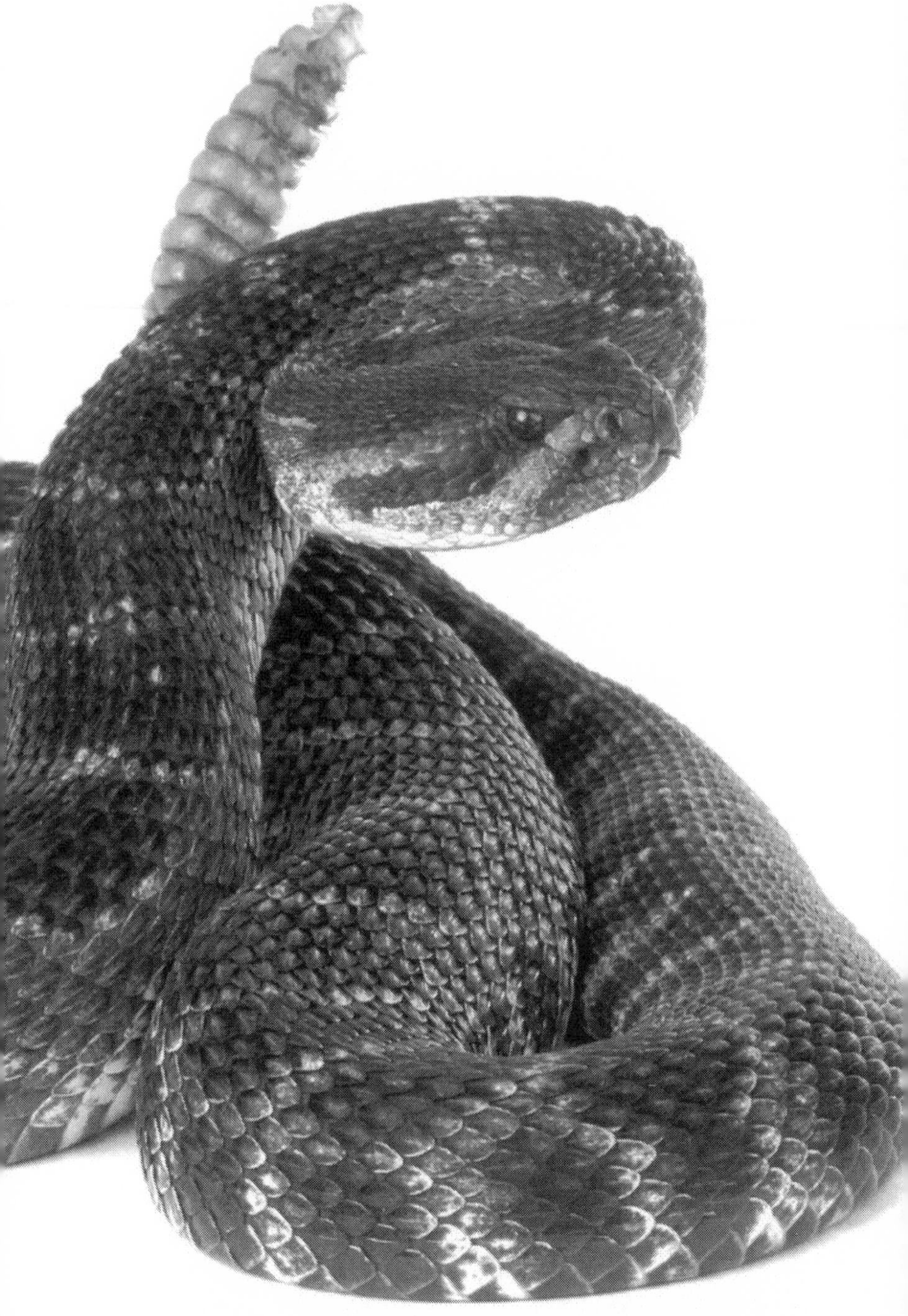

Fun Facts: Rattlesnakes

How Big Are They?

It depends on the species. The Eastern Diamondback Rattlesnake is the largest venomous snake in North America. They can grow eight feet long and weigh up to 10 pounds.

The Rattle

Rattlesnakes use their rattle to warn predators not to get too close. If you hear a rattle, slowly back away.

Unfortunately, you can't rely on the sound of a rattle to warn you that a rattlesnake is nearby. Sometimes, their rattles break off, leaving the snake silent until new rattles are able to grow.

Avoiding Bites

Most rattlesnake bites happen because people are pestering them. If you see a snake, be respectful and give it plenty of distance.

Accidental bites often happen because people don't see the snake until they're too close. Avoid sticking your hand under rocks or in crevices that you can't see into. Pay attention to where you walk and look around before sitting for a rest.

You can protect yourself by wearing thick, tall boots and baggy clothing.

If you do see a rattlesnake or hear its rattle, back away slowly.

Rattlesnake Bites: What to do.

Call for Help

- Call for help immediately. The sooner you get antivenom, the better.

Stay Still

- After calling for help, stay as still as possible. Movement causes the venom to spread faster.

Stay Calm

- Panicking increases your heartrate, spreading venom faster.

Keep the Bite Below Your Heart

- Holding the bite below the level of your heart slows the spread of the venom. Avoid holding it above your heart because the venom will spread faster.

Remove Jewelry

- Rattlesnake bites can cause a lot of swelling. If you don't remove jewelry and tight-fitting clothes, they may get stuck and cut off circulation.

Rattlesnake Bites: What not to do

Do Not Suck Out the Venom

- Sucking the venom from a bite is not very effective and can increase the chance of infection. Cutting a bitten area first to bleed out the venom or to make sucking the blood easier causes more tissue damage and infection risk.

Do Not Apply a Tourniquet

- Chances are you won't be able to get a tourniquet on fast enough to keep the venom from reaching the heart. Even if you do, it concentrates the venom in a small area, instead of diluting it throughout the blood stream. This, along with the lack of fresh blood to the limb, can cause severe tissue damage and may require the limb to be amputated.

Do Not Wash the Bite

- Doctors can collect venom samples from the skin and use them to identify what type of antivenom you need. Washing the area can remove the venom from the skin, making it hard for samples to be collected.

Would You Survive the Desert?

Water

Do not travel in the desert without lots of water. This may seem like a no-brainer, but many people lose their lives each year because they don't pack enough H2O. One water bottle or canteen will not keep you alive long in a hot desert.

Staying Cool

Normally, you might be able to survive a couple of days without water, but in hot weather, you're lucky to survive a day. That's because your body sweats to stay cool, and the more you sweat, the more water your body needs to survive.

Finding other ways to stay cool can save your life. Lying in the shade during the day and moving during the night is best. Even simple things like wearing a hat to block the sun can help prevent sweating and water loss.

Dehydration

Dehydration is what occurs when your body doesn't have as much water as it needs. Thirst, light headedness, a dry mouth, and dark urine are common signs of dehydration and should not be ignored. Unless your body gets the water it needs, dehydration can progress and cause rapid heart rates, dizziness, fainting, and even death.

Gross Fact: Drinking pee may save lives.

It may sound disgusting, but many people claim to have saved themselves from dehydration by drinking their own pee.

Is it safe to drink pee?

Normally it's safe, at least for a while. Consecutively collecting and drinking pee a few times is probably fine, but eventually toxins within the pee will become concentrated and harmful.

Does pee really prevent dehydration?

Probably, after all, pee is mostly made of water. However, some argue that those who have survived dehydration by drinking pee would have also survived without the pee. Since there's no way to prove that it was the pee that kept these people alive, the debate continues.

What we do know is that some people have survived a surprisingly long time when drinking pee, and that many of these pee-drinking survivors swear that it saved their lives.

So, should I drink my pee?

That's your call. Obviously, this technique should only be used in emergency situations, when no other water is available. But please let me know if it does save your life, because that's one story I would like to hear about.

Don't worry. As far as I know, there is no such thing as Diet Pee. I just thought this picture was better than posting a real image of pee.

Places to Find Water

- Look for water in low-lying areas.
- Try digging. Water may be just below the surface.
- Green vegetation can indicate moisture.
- Collect dew in the morning.
- Catch basins can hold water for months.
- Create a solar still.

What is a Solar Still?

A solar still traps moisture, collects condensation, and if built properly can use gravity to allow water droplets to fall into a drinking container. Most types of solar stills require a sheet of plastic to be draped over a hole that is dug into the ground. www.karlsteam.com/books/surviving-desert-view/ has a video that shows how this works.

Water in food

Some foods contain a lot of fluid. In the desert, a prickly pear cactus is an example of this. The fruit and even the pads contain water, which is why eating them can prevent dehydration.

Other foods don't contain much water. Dry cereal and beef jerky for instance. Eating dry foods can make dehydration worse, because they force your body to use its own water to digest them. Since you can survive longer without food than water, it's better not to eat dry food until you have something to drink with them.

Heatstroke

Heatstroke occurs when a body cannot cool itself properly. Hot weather and strenuous activity are often the cause. Dehydration plays a role too, because it's harder for the body to stay cool when it doesn't have enough water to produce sweat.

Heatstroke can cause your body temperature to rise to over 104 F. Your heart may race and you may breathe fast shallow breaths as your body tries to cool itself. Flushed skin, vomiting, confusion and fainting are also common signs.

To treat a heatstroke, do what it takes to cool the body. Find a place of shade or a cool breeze. If available, place cold water or ice on the skin. If a heatstroke victim remains too hot for too long, organs will begin to shut down and the person could die.

Staying Warm

Most deserts are known for their hot days, but temperatures can quickly drop during the night. In fact, of all the places on Earth, deserts have some of the greatest temperature swings from day to night. So, having fire starting tools with you and being able to find shelter is important.

Shelters

A good shelter can keep you cool during the day and keep you warm at night. The rock overhang or cave that was used in this story is a good example of this. It provided shade and kept the characters cool, but at night it could have helped to block wind and harsh weather.

How Karl Steam feels when you remember to leave a nice review.

Andrey_Kumin/Bigstock.com

★★★★☆
Another good book, but I wish they had seen a scorpion.

★★★★★
I love this series!

★★★★★
Didn't want to stop reading. Can't wait to start book 3.

★★★★☆
I liked it.

The way he feels when you forget.

PHOTOCREO Michal Bednarek/Bigstock.com

<u>Reviews Are Easy</u>

1. Choose a rating.

2. Explain your reason.
<small>(It can be as short as a sentence.)</small>

Made in the USA
Columbia, SC
06 December 2018